Dear Genevieve,

Enjoy Tobias and the history of our region.

Cookie Schultz

August 29, 2019

Tobias: The Mouse in the Old Stone House

Mary Louise "Cookie" Soldo Schultz

illustrated by Ashley Teets

Headline Kids
an imprint of Headline Books, Inc.
Terra Alta, WV

Tobias: The Mouse in the Old Stone House

by Mary Louise "Cookie" Soldo Schultz

illustrated by Ashley Teets

To order additional copies of this book, or for book publishing information, or to contact the author:

Headline Kids
P. O. Box 52
Terra Alta, WV 26764

Tel: 800-570-5951
Email: mybook@headlinebooks.com
www.headlinebooks.com
www.headlinekids.com

Service League of Morgantown
313 Chesnut St
Morgantown, WV 26505
www.OldStoneHouseWV.org

Published by Headline Books
Headline Kids is an imprint of Headline Books

ISBN-13: 978-1-88265821-3

Library of Congress Control Number: 2014954778

PRINTED IN THE UNITED STATES OF AMERICA

Dedication

Grandparents know the joy of discovering imaginary secret places with their grandchildren. Each in his or her own way, my grandchildren Matt, Allie, Kate, Stephen and Molly has contributed to the creative imagination of this tale. My family, and especially my daughters Sara and Stephie, have offered perceptive insights into the inventive minds of children. Finally, my husband Bernie, who is my deepest source of comfort, took on the voices of all the characters and, most especially, of a curious cat named Charlie who will appear in book two of this series. To all of you, as always, I give my love and thanks.

Introduction

The enchanting story of *Tobias The Mouse in the Old Stone House*, was envisioned as a way to interest children in history and to inspire curiosity about their surroundings.

In his story, Tobias shares the adventures of his ancestors who have inhabited the same house in Morgantown, West Virginia since the latter half of the eighteenth century. His account delightfully weaves the story of his family with historical facts associated with the town's prosperous growth.

Tobias' home in the actual Old Stone House is located at 313 Chestnut Street. Records suggest this sandstone dwelling was built prior to 1795 by Jacob Nuze. It is the oldest stone dwelling in Monongalia County, West Virginia and is included on the National Register of Historic Places.

Since 1935, the Old Stone House has served as the headquarters of the Service League of Morgantown. This non-profit organization maintains a gift shop year-round on the premises operated solely by volunteers. Proceeds from sales are donated to cultural and charitable concerns that benefit the citizens of Monongalia County.

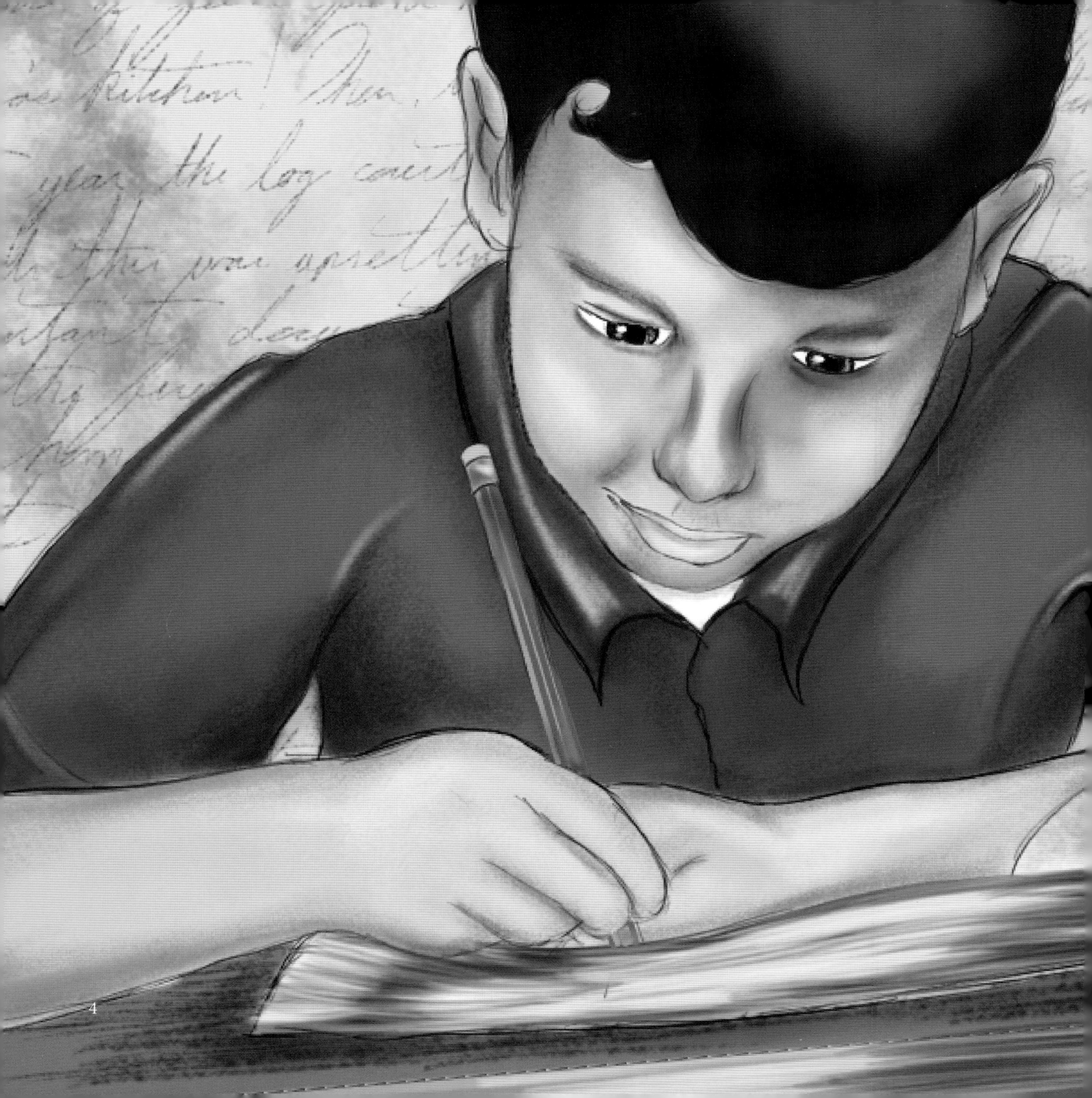

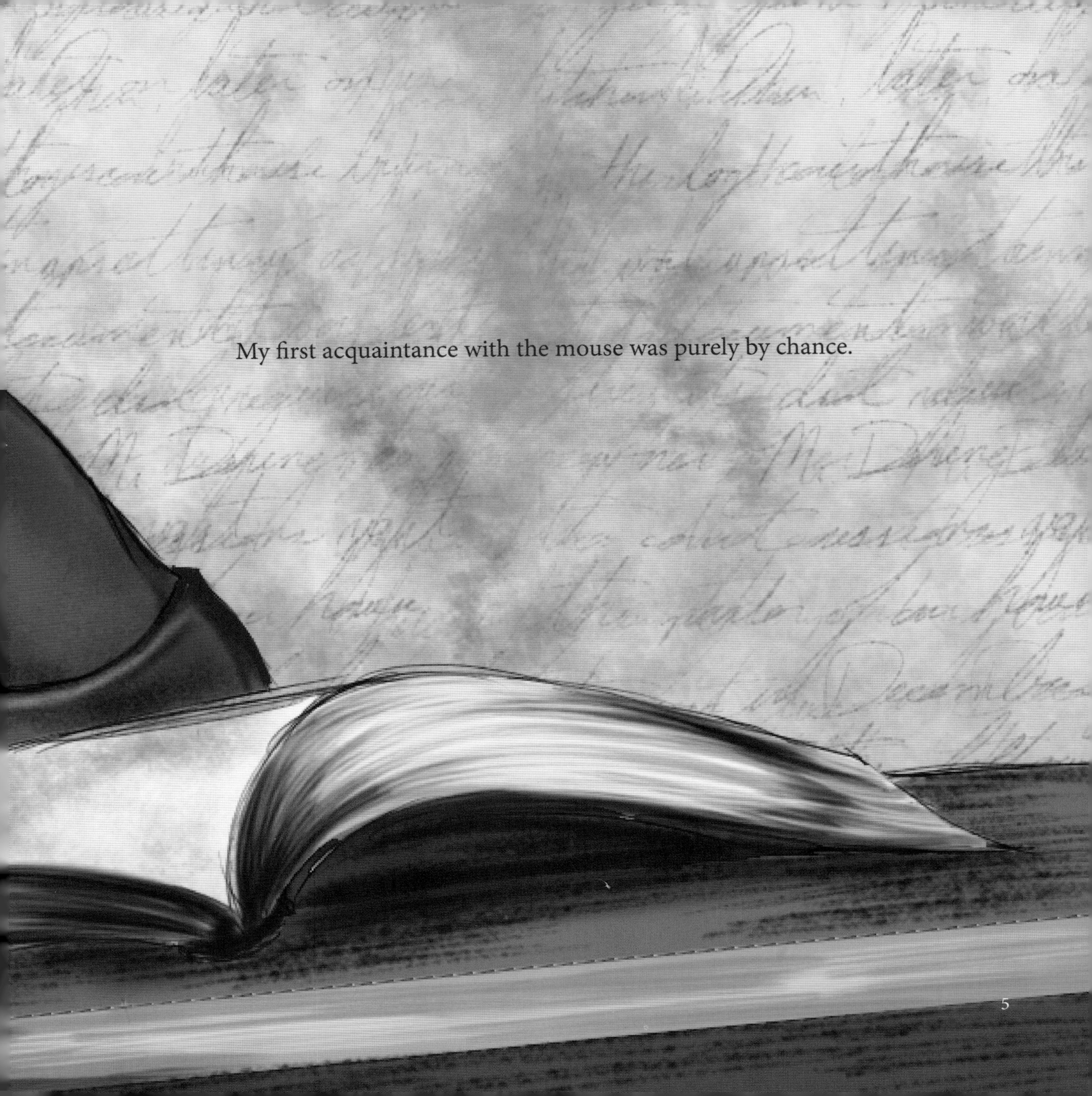

My first acquaintance with the mouse was purely by chance.

One morning in early June my grandmother, "Nonny," brought me to a gift shop in a tiny house with two front doors. Nonny said the Old Stone House was over 200 years old. She volunteered there and asked me if I would like to go with her.

7

When she unlocked the front door, I was amazed to see a cozy room filled with lots of gifts. As I looked around the room, I noticed to the left of the front door, a very narrow staircase leading to the second floor. Across the room there was a large stone fireplace, almost big enough for me to sit in. To the right, I saw a cabinet that held a worn family Bible studies book, some old bent eyeglasses and lots of broken plates. I wondered why someone would have saved broken glasses and old pieces of pottery.

The ceiling was much lower than my ceiling at home and had a thick beam running through the middle. The floor had many square nails pounded into the wide, uneven wooden boards.

8

Nonny interrupted my wanderings and asked if I would like to work on a puzzle at a table in the backroom while she opened the shop. I was so very happy to be with her. We were having a special day together, and as I soon discovered, it was to become even more special.

After a while, I got tired of my puzzle and decided to look around the front room since there weren't any customers at the moment.

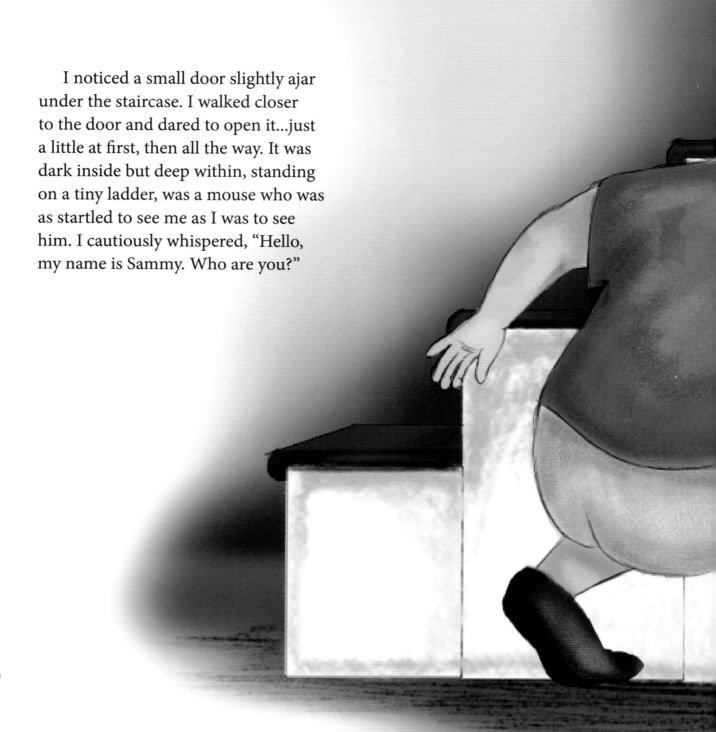

I noticed a small door slightly ajar under the staircase. I walked closer to the door and dared to open it...just a little at first, then all the way. It was dark inside but deep within, standing on a tiny ladder, was a mouse who was as startled to see me as I was to see him. I cautiously whispered, "Hello, my name is Sammy. Who are you?"

"Hello, Sammy. My name is Tobias and I live here."
As my eyes adjusted to the light in his room, I could
see Tobias was surrounded by paintings and pictures
of other mice and places in Morgantown.
"Who are all of these mice?" I asked politely.
"These are all of my ancestors who have lived under
this staircase. We have been living here in this old stone
house for over 200 years," Tobias replied. Would you
like to come in and have a cup of tea?"

13

I squeezed in and sat on the floor beside his chair. Tobias was a fairly old mouse with long gray whiskers. His red scarf accented his gray coat. There was a tiny wooden walking stick resting next to him on the chair. I could smell the tangy aroma of orange spice tea and was happy to accept a cup. Tobias explained to me the tea was a specialty of the Old Stone House and from time to time, after the ladies of the Service League left, he would pull a package of tea back into his home. He especially liked the flavors of cinnamon and cloves and, after my first sip, I agreed with him. What a mouthwatering welcome!

Old Stone House Spiced Tea Service League of Morgantown

1 (1 lb. 2 oz.) jar of Tang
1 (3 oz.) pkg. lemonade mix
2/3 cup instant tea
1/2 cup white sugar
1/4 cup brown sugar
1 tsp. ground cinnamon and 1/2 tsp. ground cloves

Combine all ingredients and mix well. Store in an airtight container. To serve, mix 1 to 2 tablespoons of mixture in a cup of boiling water.

"As I started to say," Tobias continued, "we have been here for many generations and witnessed much of the history of Morgan's Town, as Morgantown was originally called."

"When did your family arrive?" I asked.

"And how did they travel here?"

"They hitched a ride on a conestoga wagon and arrived in Morgan's Town about 1780. They found this sturdy stone house on lot #25 Long Alley* and we have been here ever since!"

*Long Alley became Middle Alley and is now known as Chestnut St.

14

15

16

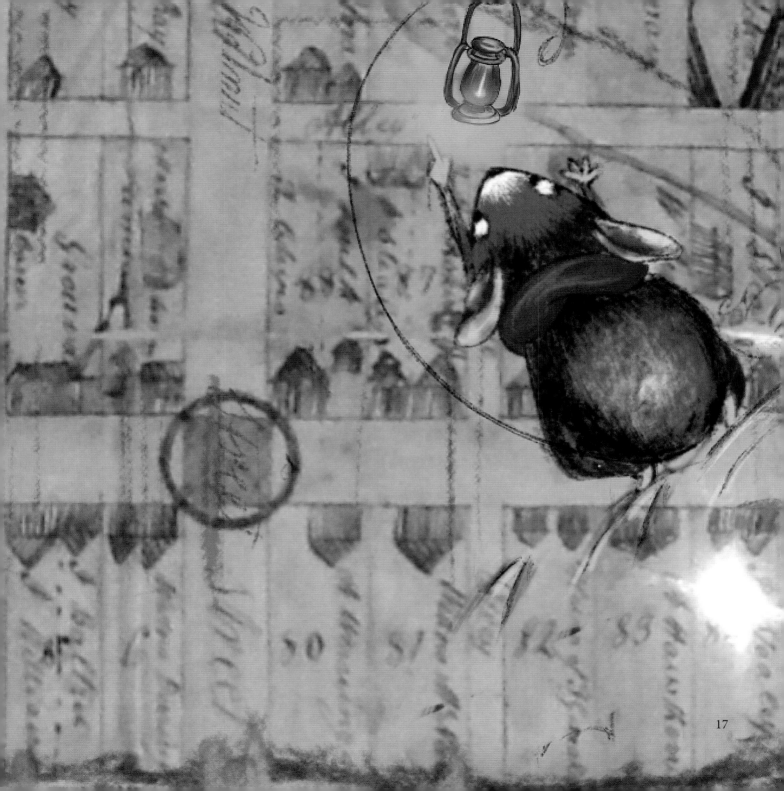

As Tobias was telling me about his ancestors I started to worry Nonny might be missing me so I begged his forgiveness and left.

"Please come back soon," Tobias said, "and when you do, I will share with you our family journal."

I slipped out through the door and quickly returned to my puzzle. Nonny was talking to a customer and hadn't even noticed my absence. When the customer left, we shared an orange and talked about how we were going to spend the rest of our afternoon. Before long the bell at the front door jingled, announcing another customer and as soon as Nonny was busy, I tiptoed back to Tobias' house under the stairs.

Tobias was waiting for me with a large
and much worn family journal. I was soon
to learn how so many of his ancestors
were a part of the history of this house
and of Morgantown.

"Come sit here on the floor beside my chair," Tobias said,
"and we can look through my journal together."

The first few pages were dated from 1805 and were written
by a mouse named Isaac. Although they were quite yellow
and faded, Tobias adjusted his monocle and began to read.

Dear Journal,

My wife Sarah and I have been living here ever since Jacob Nuze moved with his wife, Elizabeth, and their three children from their lonely farm on Aaron's Creek into this beautiful stone house. I remember hearing Elizabeth say that at last she felt safe from Indian attacks with a cistern right here in our cellar and windows on the third floor that could help us to defend our dwelling. She found it so much easier to manage her household with shops nearby like Thomas Laidley's mercantile shop and Frederic Gibler's tannery.

Sarah and I have been fortunate enough to share many fond memories of Morgan's Town. I was a bit more adventurous in those days, much to Sarah's dismay! I recall one adventure back in 1784 when I hid in Zack Morgan's wagon as he traveled out to John Pierpont's house near the Cheat River. Zack, who was the founder of our town, was meeting with Captain Samuel Hanway, the surveyor of Monongalia County, and George Washington. Can you imagine our excitement as we anticipated meeting the great hero of the Revolutionary War? General Washington was here to discuss the development of a better system of transportation from the Potomac River to the Ohio River. His plan was not fulfilled, but it was such an honor to be in the presence of this great man! We did not know it then but General Washington was soon to become our first President!

Jacob and Elizabeth seemed happy in this little house until, one day, Sarah overheard them discussing the sale of the house, for 30 pounds, to a Mr. Henry Dering. By the end of January of 1795, Henry, his wife Rebecca and their children had moved into our little home. We welcomed their arrival and the merriment that they provided as we all were recovering from the recent death of our beloved founder, Zack Morgan, on New Year's Day. The Derings were quite well known in Morgan's Town as they had opened up a tavern at the corner of High Street and Walnut Street when they arrived in 1787. Between the scraps of food George, Maria, Harriet, Henry and Sophia dropped here in the house and what we could gather from their tavern, Sarah and I were more easily able to feed our growing family. Sadly, not only did the log courthouse burn down in 1796—Dering's tavern also burned the same year. They soon replaced it and I must add, that not only were Rebecca and Henry rebuilding their tavern, they were also building quite a large family! What wonderful sounds we heard coming from the two bedrooms upstairs when their son William was born in 1797, followed by John two years later and finally by Frederick just three years ago in 1802. Mrs. Dering now owns a slave named Sawney who is helping her with her daily chores. This has given Rececca a little more time to spend instructing her children and we, too, are learning from her lessons. My Sarah has been quite attentive to Rebecca's needlework instructions to her daughters and is now making a sampler of her own with our beautiful stone home surrounded by a row of letters, numbers and some lovely birds and flowers. I am so proud of my wife! She can also count among her new found accomplishments an interest in penmanship. Sarah practices every day with her quill pen in her own book that she modeled on the

ones Rebecca made for her own eight children. Our house is filled with joy and the only fear that we have are those times when we hear feet approaching our hiding places. It is these moments when we scurry back to the safety of our room under the staircase.

We have also been quite proud of Mr. Dering of late as he has been the contractor for the construction of our new courthouse. He was very busy with this project which began in 1801 and was just completed two years ago in 1803. During this time, the sheriff asked Mr. Dering to hold two court sessions in his tavern. Our town is growing and changing so rapidly. Why now, directly across from our house, Mr. Fauquier McRa has built a house which he is also operating as a tavern. It is in a wonderful location on Walnut Street and is just up from the river. Sarah and I rarely have to worry about feeding our family with these taverns so nearby!

There has been so much to record in this first journal. The soft light of my candle will not last much longer and I feel that slumber is fast approaching. I will try to add to the history of my family and of Morgan's Town in a short while. As I read over these first few lines, I recognize how blessed my Sarah and I have been to be a part of the growth of this new town and of the two families who have lived here in our cozy stone house on Long Alley.

Isaac

May 19, 1805

Dear Journal,

The distant call of the whippoorwill has begun and through the windows the stars, those tiny treasures of the night, are lending a warm glow to the Dering's parlor. There is very little foot traffic now. The usual hustle and bustle of daily life in our frontier town of about 60 houses has ceased. John Thompson's tailor shop, John Shisler's wagon works and John Protzman's cobbler shop have been closed for several hours. If our house was situated closer to the river, we might be able to hear the quiet sounds of the water lapping against the dock at the foot of Walnut Street. But it is not and now I hear only a whisper of sound within our home and the sound of the night birds without.

This is my favorite time of the day as I begin to gather my thoughts like the pieces of a quilt. A fortnight ago, when I wrote my first entry, I forgot to mention that in October of 1785, Sarah and I were out enjoying the first hint of autumn with our newborn son, James, when we saw a man in brown breeches walking down Long Alley. His English was quite difficult to understand as he greeted Mrs. Nuze, who was gathering ferns along the shaded pathways near our house. With a friendly "bonjour," he said his name was Albert Gallatin and he was here in the county seat to become a naturalized citizen. Sarah, James and I hid in a nearby thicket in hopes of learning more about this man with the decidedly strange accent.

He explained he was born in Geneva, Switzerland and came to America in 1780 at the age of 19. Two years after his arrival, he accepted a position at Harvard College in Massachusetts as a French tutor but soon decided to explore the western lands of the Ohio River Valley. He liked his life on the frontier and spent the summer of 1785 in Fayette County, close to Morgan's Town. Mrs. Nuze, who was fond of hosting sociable parties, suggested he stop by for refreshments after he concluded his affairs at the courthouse.

Later in the afternoon, Mr. Gallatin was at our door. As it was a fall day, there was a slight chill in the air and Mrs. Nuze had made a fire in our stone fireplace. In front of the fire, she set an elegant table for her guest with her best blue and cream Queen's ware on a delicate hand-woven pink and white cotton cloth. We heard Mr. Gallatin praise Mrs. Nuze for her tasty ginger cookies and for the tangy pot of tea. Mrs. Nuze explained she purchased the ginger root that very morning at Mr. Laidley's store and was happy to make excellent use of it by midday! After a while, Mr. Gallatin turned his cup upside down on his saucer and Mrs. Nuze understood this was the most mannerly way for him to signal to his hostess it was time for him to take his leave. With a polite "au revoir," he was on his way. Sarah and I retreated to our home under the staircase, our hearts filled with the joy of the day.

Well, goodbye, dear reader. Before I close this journal tonight, I am pressing a tiny blue forget-me-not between these pages to remind my son, James and following generations, to continue to narrate the adventures of our mouse family.

Isaac

When Tobias looked up, he had a tear in his eye. Although he had never met Isaac or his wife Sarah, he told me he felt close to his ancestors and that it was his responsibility to preserve the family journals and the home they had created so many years ago under the staircase of the Old Stone House.

Knowing his new friend would return with his Nonny in another week, Tobias promised to share with Sammy a story about the next resident, Jacob Foulk, a potter who lived in the Old Stone House with his family.

"Sammy," Tobias said, "I can't wait to share with you the adventures of my mischievous ancestor, Nicholas, whose behavior dramatically improves with the arrival of a cat named Charlie."

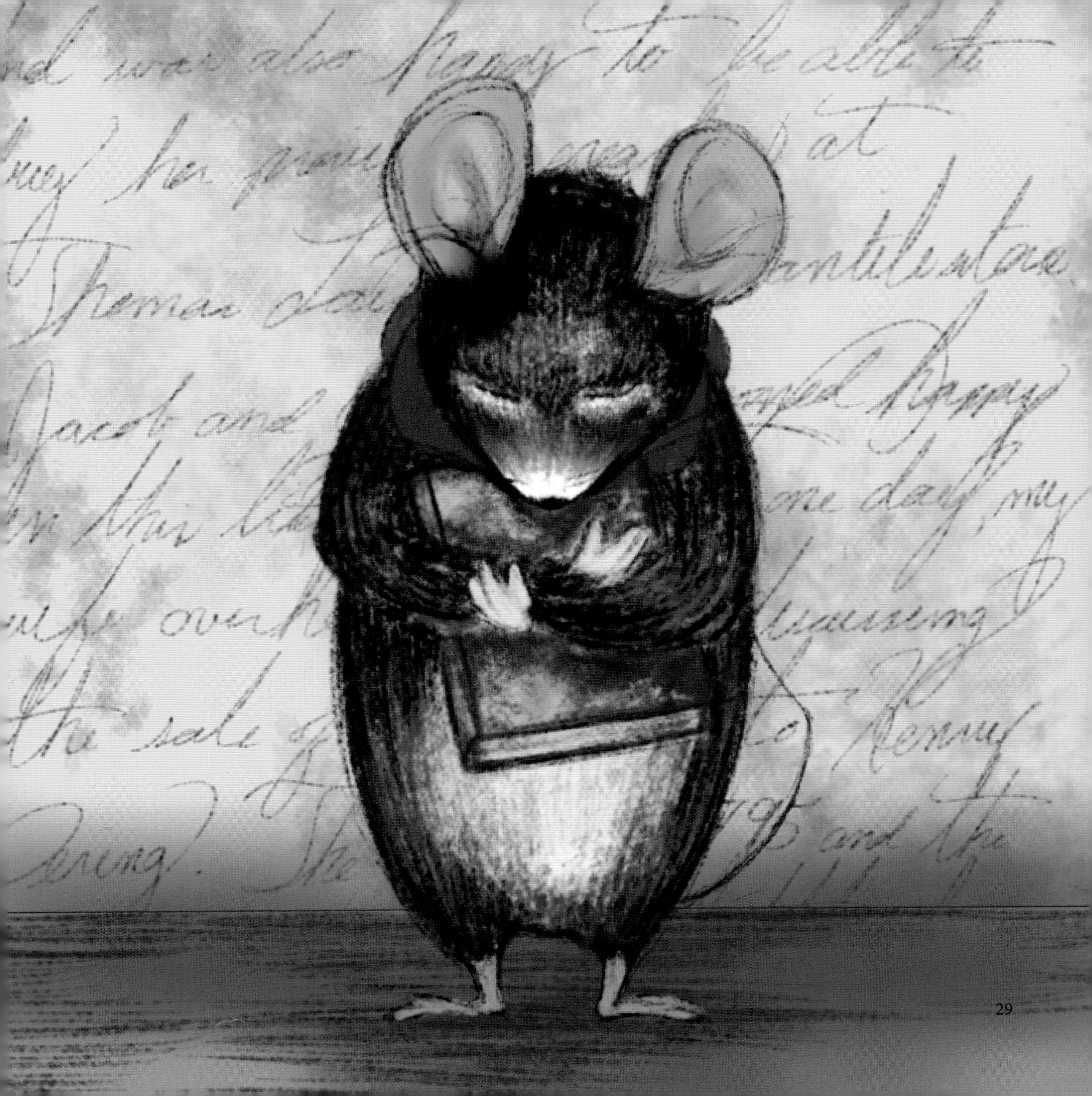

Isaac

Sarah

James

The World of the Nuze and Dering Families

ALBERT GALLATIN: Albert Gallatin (1761-1849) was the 4th Secretary of the Treasury, serving under Presidents Jefferson and Madison. While holding this office, he was instrumental in the Louisiana purchase, funded the Lewis and Clark Expedition and the War of 1812. Near his home in Fayette County, Pennsylvania, which he named Friendship Hill, he built a glass works.

CISTERN: There was no running water in Colonial America but at the Old Stone House there was a well (a cistern) in the cellar, which can still be seen today.

CONESTOGA WAGON: A covered wagon with slightly curved sides developed circa 1725 in the Conestoga region of Pennsylvania. It was used to transport goods and pioneer families primarily in Pennsylvania, Ohio, Maryland and Virginia. A feed box for animals, tool chest, and water barrel were mounted on its sides. To prevent leaks and to allow the wagon to cross streams and rivers, the spaces between the boards were sealed with tar. It was usually drawn by six horses and had wheels that rose up to six feet high and was in use until the development of trains.

PENMANSHIP: Colonial children practiced their letters in a booklet of blank pages called a copybook and wrote with a quill pen dipped in ink.

THE POUND: In the Colonial era, the monetary system included pounds, shillings and pence. Henry Dering will pay 30 pounds to Jacob Nuze for the purchase of the Old Stone House on January 28, 1795..

SAMPLERS: Educated young girls in Colonial America learned to make samplers which usually featured the alphabet, numbers and a small picture done in either cross stitch or embroidery.

SCHOOLING FOR AFRICAN AMERICANS: In Virginia, it was illegal for slaves to be educated. Yet, here in our town, the Dering's last child, Frederick Augustus, born in 1802 in the Old Stone House, will eventually teach Sunday School to the slaves in the Monongalia Academy.

SLAVERY: It is known that Rebecca Dering had a female slave named Sawney and two male slaves, Henry and Tim. Rececca Dering in her will of 1844 made "provision for the freedom of her Negro slave, Henry at the end of two years and of her Negro boy, Tim, at the age of twenty-one."

TAVERNS: Taverns in Colonial America served as local gathering places where people met to discuss the news of the day, conduct business and chat over drinks and meals. They often provided lodging for guests as well. The state of Virginia required tavern keepers to apply for annual licenses.

Acknowledgments

I could not have completed this tale without the support of many organizations and individuals. I particularly thank the members of the Service League of Morgantown and the members of the Handcraft Committee who, along with Alison Gile, have created our Tobias merchandise.

I offer a special thank you to Diana Claydon, who not only guided the project from its inception, but was instrumental in securing funding from the John M. Brown Family Foundation and the Morgantown Convention and Visitors Bureau. We have also been fortunate to receive funding from Mylan, Inc., JoAnn Taylor, Sharon Turner, Judie Dinsmore, Carolyn Gray, Joann King, Hope Covey, Connie Bucklew, Vicki Auch, Carol Loar, Martha DeLo, Joan Bissett, Marva Graff, Jeanne Grimm, Carolyn Keech, Doris Reed, Rama Riemenschneider, Jan Mitchell, Kathleen Dyer, Cheryl Heflin, Alice Frost, Kristin Valenti, Susan Dotson, Gale Truman, Charlotte Dalton and Shalane Koon.

To recreate the world in which Tobias' ancestors live, I am indebted to scholarly works written by Earl Core, Samuel Wiley, James Callahan, Connie Rice and Norma Venable.

I offer a heart felt thank you to Kay Goodwin, Cabinet Secretary, West Virginia Department of Education and the Arts, for her endorsement of this project.

Previous histories of the Old Stone House were invaluable to me and I especially recognize the work of Iris Smith, Leoan Crowe, Anita Ball and Judie Dinsmore, author of the Bicentennial History of the Old Stone.

I recognize the following who have lent authoritative understanding to this tale: historians Barbara Rasmussen and Barbara Howe, Pamela Ball, Richard McEwuen and Michael Mackert from the Morgantown History Museum, Christy Venham and Stewart Plein from the West Virginia and Regional History Center, Dick Walters from the Monongalia Historical Society and Gary Friggens from the Josephine and William Aull Center, Laura Savio, Joann King, Roger and Charlotte Dalton, Kathy Hanko, Alice and Jack Frost, Janet Rogers, Sue Carpenter, Joan Bissett, Marlene Pope, Holly Loar and Kristin Valenti.

I am especially grateful to Ashley Teets, whose charming illustrations have enlivened our narrative and to publisher Cathy Teets, President of Headline Books, Inc.

I owe a special debt of gratitude to Joe and Carol Baim, Roger Crum, Doug Rutledge, Steve Orloski, Anne Selinger Charon and my sisters, Millie Ryan and Suzy Bock, who have always offered kind support.

Finally, I owe my interest in local history to Jane Labys whose memory and friendship are always with me.

Cookie Soldo Schultz, March, 2015